My First Collection of
Animal
Stories

p

4

Tiger tricks

Tiger loved to play tricks. Every time he found a new one, he couldn't wait to try it out on all of his friends. His latest one was – tying knots!

So, when Elephant was fast asleep, Tiger tied a large knot in his trunk! When Monkey was dozing, Tiger tied a knot in his tail! And when Snake was snoozing, Tiger tied a knot – in Snake!

Tiger thought it was great fun. The other animals didn't – they were fed up with Tiger and his tricks.

5

"I've had enough of this!" said Elephant, rubbing his sore trunk.

"Something has to be done," said Monkey, rubbing his sore tail.

"He's gone too far this time!" said sore Snake.

6

"We need to catch him before he can try out any more of his tricks on us," said Monkey.

"But that's the problem," said Snake. "We never see him coming in time."

The others agreed. They never spotted Tiger sneaking up on them, because, in the jungle, Tiger's stripes made him really difficult to see!

So all the animals thought really hard. Monkey scratched his head, Snake wriggled and writhed and Elephant swung his trunk.

Suddenly, Elephant said, "I've got an idea!" He led them all to a fruit tree near the water hole.

When Elephant had explained his plan, a huge smile spread across Monkey's face and Snake began to snigger.

Monkey quickly scampered up the tree and carried down some of the bright red fruits. Snake wriggled around in the soft earth, until he made a smooth hollow. Then, Elephant squeezed the fruits with his trunk, until the bright red juice filled the hollow that Snake had made – and then the animals waited.

It wasn't long before Tiger came strolling along to the water hole, giggling. He started drinking...

Elephant dipped his trunk into the fruit juice and sucked hard. Then, he pointed his trunk at Tiger and blew.

The juice flew across the clearing, spattering Tiger all over, soaking into his coat. He looked as if he had bright red spots! Tiger jumped with shock.

"That'll take weeks to wear off," said Elephant.

"We'll see you coming for miles," said Monkey.

"So you won't be able to sneak up on us and play any more tricks," added Snake.

And all the animals laughed – except for bright red Tiger!

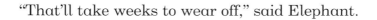

Please tell me why

"Come on, tortoise!" says my Mum,
When I'm too slow getting dressed.
Can't she see that I don't wear a shell
And that all I have on is my vest?

Dad calls me a mischievous monkey,
But I don't see how that can be.
I don't have a tail, I'm not covered in fur,
Though I'm quite good at climbing, you see.

Mum calls me "night owl", when I cannot sleep,
Though I don't hoot and I don't have wings.
And I certainly do not have feathers
And owls must have all of those things.

It's true that I slither into their bed,
'Cos I like to say, "Hi!" when I wake.
But my skin isn't scaly, so please tell me why
Dad says, "Here comes that wriggly snake"?

It's not fair!

"I want to swim with the ducklings," said Kitten to Mother Cat, as they walked past the pond.

"You can't," Mother Cat told her. "Your fur isn't waterproof like ducklings' feathers. Kittens aren't meant to swim."

"It's not fair!" grumbled Kitten. "Ducklings have all the fun!"

"I want to roll in the mud with the piglets," said Kitten, as they walked past the pigsty.

"You can't," Mother Cat told her. "Piglets have quite smooth skin. Your long fur will get knotted and matted with the mud. Kittens aren't meant to roll in mud."

"It's not fair!" moaned Kitten. "Piglets have all the fun!"

"I want to fly with the baby birds," said Kitten to Mother Cat, as Kitten tried climbing the tree, where Mother Sparrow was giving her babies some flying lessons.

"You can't," Mother Cat told her. "You have fur, not feathers and you haven't got wings. Kittens aren't meant to fly."

16

"It's not fair!" shouted Kitten. "Birds have all the fun!" And she stamped her paws on the ground.

"Don't worry," said Mother Sparrow, hopping up to Mother Cat. "I've got an idea. I'll see you later."

In the farm kitchen, Kitten curled up on a rug by the fire, with a saucer of milk.

"I want to sleep by the fire," said a duckling, waddling past the open door.

"You can't," said his mother. "Ducklings can't sleep by fires!"

"I want to lie on a rug," said a piglet, trotting past the door.

18

"You can't," said his mother. "You'd get it covered with mud!"

"I want to drink a saucer of milk," said a baby bird, swooping past the window.

"You can't," said his mother. "Birds don't drink milk!"

"It's not fair!" said Duckling, Piglet and Baby Bird, together.

"Oh, yes, it is!" mewed Kitten, smiling!

19

20

My hamster

My hamster tears up paper,
'Cos that's what hamsters do.
He isn't being naughty,
But hamsters like to chew!

It causes lots of trouble
And everyone gets mad.
"Who ate my daily paper
And made this mess?" yells Dad.

My Mum starts cooking dinner,
Then shouts, "Just come and look!
Your hamster's chewed a hole
Right through my cookery book!"

My brother's homework's missing.
It's in my hamster's cage.
My hamster is quite happy.
My brother's in a rage!

My hamster just chews paper
To make himself a nest.
So why are they all shouting,
"That hamster is a pest!"

21

Hide and seek

"You can be 'It', Daisy," said Alex. "You count and we'll hide."

"Okay," said Daisy. "Poppy can help me to look for you." Poppy was Daisy's new puppy.

"Don't be silly," laughed Sam. "A puppy can't play hide and seek."

"She can because… " began Daisy. But the others weren't listening. They had all run off across the field to hide.

"Never mind, Poppy," Daisy told her puppy. "You'll just have to sit here and be good."

23

Daisy turned round to face the tree. She closed her eyes and began to count; "… ninety-eight, ninety-nine, one hundred." That should have given everyone long enough to hide. Daisy looked around the field. There was no one to be seen. Poppy whined as Daisy ran off towards the hole in the hedge, where they had made a den.

She found Sam almost straight away.
He was tucked down in a corner of the den.
She took him back to the tree. Poppy
whined at them.

"Dogs can't play hide and seek," Sam told
the puppy and tickled her ear. "You can sit
here with me."

25

Then Daisy found Sarah and
Michael just as easily. Emily was
harder to find – she was lying very
still in the long grass at the end of the
field. Her green t-shirt and trousers
made her difficult to see. Daisy took
her back to the tree, where the others
were all waiting. Poppy whined each
time she came back.

"Shhh!" said Daisy. "I won't be long
now." But Daisy was wrong – she
couldn't find Alex anywhere! Daisy
had looked in all their favourite hiding
places, but he wasn't in any of them.
She didn't know what to do.

"We'll help you to find Alex," said Michael.

So the children searched every corner of the field and every bit of the hedge, but Alex couldn't be found anywhere.

Then, Poppy began to whine louder.

"She's trying to tell us something," said Daisy.

Poppy jumped up. She ran to the tree trunk, leapt up and began barking. The children all looked up and there was Alex, sitting on a branch above them, laughing!

"See!" he said. "Daisy was right – puppies can play hide and seek."